RAMSES II

RAMSES II

Mark A. Simpkins
and
Susan Taylor

Simpkins Splendor of Egypt
SALT LAKE CITY

Simpkins Splendor of Egypt
P.O. Box 17072
Salt Lake City, Utah 84117 U.S.A.

Printed in the United States of America
First Edition

9 8 7 6 5 4 3

ISBN 0-916095-10-X

Photographs by Don Busath M. Photog., Cr., CPP, F-ASP

To Anna Fletcher

A seated, black granite colossus of Ramses II. The Court of Ramses II, Temple of Amun, Luxor Temple.

Chapter 1

INTRODUCTION

Hidden deep within the mysteries of ancient Egypt are the inner thoughts of her people, the hopes and fears behind the facade of public announcements and events. We can learn a certain amount from surviving letters and inscriptions. These indicate that the ancient Egyptians were people much like us — concerned about living a good life, happy for small pleasures, and at times, aggravated by employers and neighbors.

However, just as we never completely know ourselves, we can never fully understand the inner nature of even such famous — and well-documented — men as Ramses II. The records of his reign are not at fault — they are extensive. Ramses' every pronouncement was followed by a flurry of writing and record-keeping. With the ancient Egyptians' love of counting things, we know much about him, even the number of cakes, fish, and loaves he used at each great state celebration.

And yet Ramses remains a mystery. We know that at age fifteen he had fought in battle. At twenty-five he had married several times and had fathered at least

1

fourteen children. He was quite possibly the pharaoh who was persuaded by Moses to allow the Hebrews to leave Egypt. And yet none of these remarkable events can tell us who he really was or what spurred him to carve his place in history.

Ramses' strength as a man and as a leader is evident. He lived to the age of ninety, ruling majestically at least sixty-five years. His years as pharaoh (1290-1224 B.C.) marked a period of prosperity and security for Egyptians of every class. He was ambitious, both for himself and for his country. In at least one decisive moment of great courage he not only saved himself from death, but became a hero who could act as a peacemaker for his people as well. His deep love for his family, especially his tenderness towards his young sons and daughters, spilled over into a concern for his administrators and laborers.

But Ramses also comes down through history as a man both stubborn and vain. Ramses was not a man cut from the same humble cloth as an Abraham Lincoln. He built grandiose temples extolling his own virtues in the most flowery and inflated language. He exalted himself and insisted that his subjects know he was the nearest thing to a God.

With all of his complexities, Ramses II was the ideal of generations of Egyptians who followed him. He was to become a legend in Herodotus's Tales of the Middle East, and centuries later his was a major role in Cecil B. Demille's *The Ten Commandments*. Records suggest he would have been pleased to see himself appearing before millions of people, idealized and made larger than life.

The following pages are based on known facts, and yet must contain some speculation. Ramses was Egypt's most prolific builder, and one of her longest reigning pharaohs. From Abydos to Abu Simbel his unmistakable mark is ever present. Ramses' life exemplified the grandeur of his times. Egyptians knew him as a soldier, scholar, law-giver and god, and perhaps as the great pharaoh of Moses' day. *Ramses II* is an informal look at the unfolding of a pharaoh's life — his times, his victories, his defeats, and his family.

Two Nile gods bind the symbols representing Upper (lotus) and Lower (papyrus) Egypt into the "sma," the hieroglyphic for "union." Above, the cartouche of Ramses II. Temple of Ramses II at Abu Simbel.

Chapter 2

THE BIRTH OF A PHARAOH

The naming of a child — and more importantly a child destined to become pharaoh of Egypt — is a special event. In Ramses' time names themselves were very important. The ancient Egyptians believed that speaking and writing were sacred forms of creation. They could make something so by saying it was so. A hieroglyphic, it was believed, created an object that would actually exist in the "Netherworld." A child's name, so often written and spoken throughout his life, could make the difference between happiness and sorrow, a long life or a short one. Egyptian parents often sought to start their children out on the best footing possible by naming them for, and placing them under the protection of, the gods. Ramses' parents were no exception.

Ramses did not come from a long line of royal blood. His grandfather, Ramses I, a native of the northern delta, started out as an army officer and steadily worked his way to the position of Chief Minister of State. As a reward for his loyalty and integrity, he was appointed to the crown by the childless Pharaoh Haremhab.

Young Ramses' parents, then, may have felt that he needed the special protection which had brought his grandfather good fortune. There were no family names in those times, so the infant was named simply "Ramses," meaning "born of Re, the great sun-god." It was a name that would serve him well, but he would not always be content with it. He was to adopt many different official names in his lifetime, and to rename his wives and children when he wanted to change their status or function.

Egyptians in Ramses' time valued families highly and were very open in their love and affection for children. Large families were encouraged, and they provided a nurturing environment where parents and children expressed their feelings freely. Parents included children in "adult" activities, paid attention to their stories, and hugged and played with them tenderly. This was true for daughters as well as sons. Often daughters accompanied their fathers on hunting trips and other "manly" events.

Before Ramses was born, his parents, Seti and Tuya, had given birth to a son, who died in infancy, and to a daughter, Tjia. Ramses, the third born, was thereby destined to step into his father's footsteps. Later, another sister, Hentmire, joined the family.

Ramses got along well with his sisters. He was to later make Tjia's husband a senior official in his administration. Perhaps it was from his sisters as a youth that he learned to get along so well with women, for he was to have a model marriage with the famous and beautiful Nefertari, his chief consort.

We have no record of his playing with his childhood friends. However, Ramses was later to bring his childhood peers into his administration and to depend upon their advice and help. He made and kept good friends, both at home and abroad.

Throughout their lives Ramses was devoted to his parents, especially his mother, Tuya. She was a quiet and kind woman who shied from taking part in affairs of state. She had been a princess of royal blood before her marriage to Seti, thus ensuring that their son would be heir to the throne. Ramses' father had a more mercurial nature, and set about to educate his son in the ways of a king at an early age.

Seti I holds a censur while his son, Ramses II, wearing the sidelock of youth, recites hymns from a papyrus roll in front of the well-known king list. Gallery of Kings, Temple of Seti I at Abydos.

Chapter 3

YOUNG RAMSES IN BATTLE

The first officially heralded event in Ramses' life was his appointment at age ten as Commander-In-Chief of the army. Although this may seem young, the appointment was not out of character for his father, Seti I (Sethos). Seti had built his reputation as a great warrior and was renowned for relishing battle and decapitating his enemies. Seti's father (Ramses I) had also distinguished himself in the armed services, rising through the ranks of the elite chariot-corps. The young Ramses had a strong military image to live up to.

Eventually Ramses did live up to that image. However, it appears that — despite his early appointment — Ramses probably did not take part in an actual battle until he was in his mid-teens, sheltered even then from the worst of the fray. Ramses was included in the commemoration scene of this first battle only as an afterthought, squeezed into the scene with some difficulty.

It was not considered odd for a king to introduce his sons to battle at an early age. Ramses himself introduced his sons to war when they were still quite small.

As Egypt had struggled to dominate other countries, the soldier had become a cult hero, replacing the wise, pacifist administrator as an ideal. Scribes in Ramses' time constantly preached against soldiering, but with little effect. Young boys looked forward to the adventures the battlefield held. It was considered proper for the young Ramses to get a good head start on his future duties as Commander-In-Chief.

Young Ramses took part in several battles. Egypt was beset with small revolutions in its outer provinces, which called for immediate attention, and pirates along the Mediterranean coast, who called for a more careful strategy. Ramses was especially proud of his role in ambushing the pirates' ships on a looting raid near the mouth of the Nile. Although the looters had been harassing the Hittites and other Mediterranean powers, it was Egypt — led by the young Prince-Regent — who finally put an end to the threat.

One battle which made a deep impression upon Ramses was his father's attempt to gain control over the city of Kadesh in nearby Syria. At one time this city had paid taxes to Egypt; however, it had been over a century since a pharaoh had received any revenue from this regional capital. The neighboring Hittites now controlled the area, but had not prepared for a battle with the super-power of the region. Seti attacked the city, Ramses in tow, and captured it.

However, it didn't take long for control of the city to revert to the Hittite emperor, Muwatallis. Muwatallis and his troops were too great in numbers and in self-discipline for Seti's men to push them aside. So Seti signed an agreement ceding Kadesh in return for a Hittite pledge to leave Egypt's southern seaports in peace. Seti may have been satisfied with the arrangement, but Ramses, with the enthusiasm of youth, set his sights on recapturing the town.

It seems that during this period Ramses acquired a taste for battle that was not particularly tempered by a sense of his own perishability. Kadesh was later to be the site of the battle in which Ramses' own carelessness nearly cost him his life.

In each battle he fought, Ramses saw captives taken, over 600 in the revolt of Irem, a southern province. He learned to use these people as slaves — an anomaly for a man who was to later treat his own workers so well. Some historians believe it was Ramses who learned — the hard way — from Moses that it was sometimes wiser to let such people go.

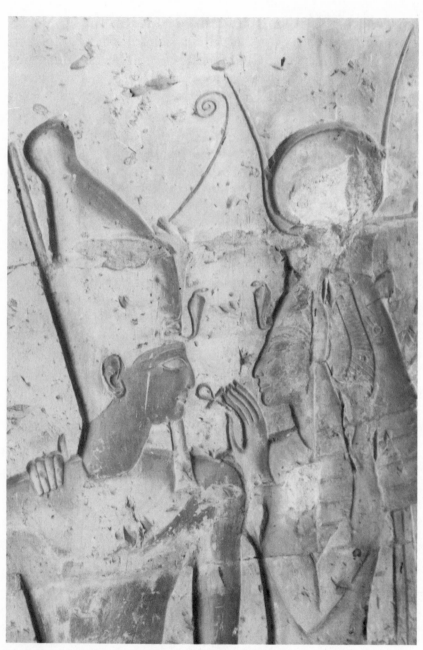

The embrace of Ramses II, Temple of Seti I at Abydos

Chapter 4

EARLY EDUCATION

Ramses' education wasn't entirely in war. He, along with the other children of the nobility, started school around the age of five, learning first to read and write. The beginner's exercise was to copy and recopy "dead Egyptian," the Latin of Ramses' day. Students then graduated to extensive word lists — places, activities, plants, and animals. When Ramses had mastered those, he copied letters written by his teachers and traditional proverbs such as, "He who tends his crop will eat it," or "Repeat only what you have seen, not what you have heard." The common wisdom of the day held that children would not learn without being disciplined, so Ramses was probably rapped on the head more than once by his tutor.

The Egyptians were very moral, and taught their children proverbs, heroic myths and solemn religious stories. Ramses was also exposed to a large collection of folk tales and wisdom.

One example of a folk tale current at the time was the tale of the doomed prince. This story was about a young prince whose destiny was an early death. All Egyptians believed that their children's fate could be foretold according to their date of birth, their first words or some other omen. In this case, the doomed prince's future was foreseen by seven goddesses, who told the king that the boy would be slain by a dog, a snake, or a crocodile. The king, hoping to outwit fortune, raised his son secluded from any living creatures. However, after many years alone the boy felt he could no longer hide from his fate and asked for a dog. The king acquiesced and the prince soon tamed it.

The prince thereafter set out to make his fortune, taking the dog with him. He entered a competition to win the hand of a princess, and won her hand by leaping higher than any other suitor. After their marriage he confessed the danger that both the snake and the crocodile still posed to them, and she promised to be vigilant in protecting him. Each night she set out a jug of wine and a jug of beer. One night a snake appeared, sipped from the jugs and became drunk. The princess grabbed a knife, chopped the snake into pieces and thus disposed of the second threat. A long period of happiness and tranquillity followed and the prince almost forgot his doom. However, one day he fled his barking dog, and came to a lake with a large crocodile.

Our record of this tale breaks off near this point. However, the story is not interrupted before the crocodile offers to spare the prince's life if he meets certain conditions. Since the Egyptians believed in the triumph of good, it is likely that the doomed prince escaped his fate.

This tale surely had its effect on a young boy,

especially if he himself was a prince. Ramses was later to display the courage, perseverance, fairness, and hope which are so evident in this childhood story.

As a young boy Ramses was exposed to the study of ancient history — thousand-year-old pyramids, ancient monuments, and museums. The looting of old tombs was a scandal even when he was young. Judging from his later actions, he was inculcated with a desire to protect his ancestors as well as his parents and himself from the inevitable looting bands.

Ramses also acquired a sense of destiny. He knew of the ancient split between Upper and Lower Egypt which had been reconciled by great kings, and of how the gods had ended their direct reign by ceding the throne to the pharaohs. Ramses knew that he was to be the "ruler of two lands," Upper and Lower Egypt, and that he must preserve a balance in attending to these regions. He was taught that the successful king divided his time between the cities of Memphis in the north and Thebes in the south.

Ramses was also taught that Egypt had seen days of greater power and prestige, and that a great leader might restore his country to her rightful place. Just a few generations before, the innovative but unwary Akhenaten had ignored the dangerous rise in power of the warrior Hittite nation (what is now Turkey). Akhenaten had lost to the Hittites one of Egypt's most important subject-states, Amurru, which included Kadesh, the city which both Seti and Ramses were to covet. Akhenaten's defeat was a humiliation to the people of Egypt. In Seti's time nationalistic feelings would probably have rivaled the feelings of the confederate south in the years after the U.S. Civil War. However, by the time Ramses came to power, the sting of defeat had at least partially healed.

Ramses prepared for the great tasks before him not only in battle but in training for administrative duties as well. He accompanied his father up and down the Nile, watching an endless procession of workers building tombs, sculpting statues and working mines. Travel was a national pastime, and he went far afield, experiencing as many new places and new people as he could.

Whether Ramses' physical stature was imposing as a child, we don't know. We do know, however, that in adulthood Ramses was tall, physically strong and full of energy. Throughout his childhood his father subjected him to rigorous exercises and constant physical activity. By the time he was a young man, he was an excellent sportsman and an accomplished athlete.

The major event in Ramses' late childhood was his coronation as Prince-Regent. Seti had decided to give Ramses a feel for the responsibilities of the throne. At an elaborate ceremony the king declared that he wanted to see his son in full splendor while he was still alive. Proclaiming his son Prince-Regent, Seti stopped just short of making him an equal partner in his own reign.

This marked the official end of Ramses' youth. After Seti's death, Ramses would speak of his father's gesture as a sign of his love. He would recall that Seti had wept at the ceremony, and would talk of how his father had protected and cared for him.

Chapter 5

THE ROYAL HAREM

Being crowned Prince-Regent meant that Ramses must establish a household, in this case, a royal harem. The harem was more than a multi-family residence and in some respects had little to do with family life at all. It was a center of culture, education and production for the large royal entourage. Members of the harem were in charge of manufacturing clothing — all of the fine linen — for the royal household. They also conducted apprenticeships in weaving and spinning, sometimes bringing in young women from other countries to learn their art.

Dress inside the harem was a product of the hard work of its residents. Clothing for royalty was unique. While peasants and workers wore only a loincloth, the nobility wore long clothes, white linen shirts and long pleated skirts, as sheer as possible to stay comfortable in the heat. Although peasants wore no shoes, royalty wore sandals, often with embedded jewels. Ramses probably had a pair of sandals with enemy nations depicted on the inner soles. Whenever he put them on, he symbolically walked on those he would govern. Royalty also wore an abundance of jewelry, each piece often weighing several pounds.

There were several harems located up and down the Nile. They were places of rest and relaxation for both the pharaoh and his family, and they were designed to provide a restful atmosphere for the residents. These impressive palaces were decorated with large quantities of gems — deep blue lapislazuli and green malachite. Flowers were raised in the royal gardens or shipped in daily to decorate and to create fragrances of every kind.

Administering the harems was a difficult and time-consuming job, and this duty was assigned to Ramses' most trusted officials. Each harem was supported through income from the vast estates which had been set aside for this very purpose. The harem estates produced cattle, milk and grain. What was not consumed was sold and the profits used for royal household expenses.

During Ramses' time women had many legal rights of their own. Men were taught to remember how hard childbirth was and to give due regard to their mothers, first, and then later to their wives. In divorce, women received one-third of the common property. While it was considered unusual, a woman could also hold government office. Queen Hatshepsut had both ruled Egypt and served as a co-regent. Other women had ruled in behalf of their sons until the young princes were old enough to reign in their own stead. The queen mother's lineage was considered to be crucial to the pharaoh's right to inherit the throne, and Ramses was to marry his own daughters, Bint-Anath and Meryetamun, later in his life to see to it that the correct succession was assured.

Although in Ramses' time some marriages were arranged, prospective grooms and brides had a great deal of choice in their mates. Apparently Ramses' father had surrounded him with young women at an early age to give him (and them) a chance to make such choices. There was no pressure for Ramses to restrict the number of women he married. To the contrary, having many children was a source of pride for a pharaoh, and he was expected to have numerous consorts. This was a royal prerogative. Although polygamy was allowed among commoners, it was rarely practiced and couples were at least nominally expected to be faithful.

Ramses fathered over 170 children — at least 111 sons and 57 daughters. We are not certain how many times he married in order to beget this large brood. However, we do know that of all his wives Ramses cherished his wife Nefertari most. Her full name was Nefertari-meri-en-mut, or "hereditary princess; mistress of both lands; beloved of the king and united with the ruler." Ramses claimed that she was among the most beautiful of all the women in the court. Ramses took her with him on trips of state, placed her at his side at hearings and ceremonies and honored her with a magnificent temple at Abu Simbel.

Ramses was close to another of his wives, Istnofret. She was an equal in rank to Nefertari, yet appears only in the background on all royal inscriptions up until the time of Nefertari's death. Istnofret probably lived in

Ramses' palace all of her life — her son Khaemwaset appears prominently throughout Ramses' life. Yet Ramses' greatest affection was reserved for Nefertari.

Nefertari had probably prepared herself long and well for marriage, if not this royal marriage. She was probably well-educated and well-travelled. We know little about her personality, but she appears as a woman of great beauty in inscriptions of the time, an indication that she was well-loved by the workmen who labored in her presence.

Chapter 6

RAMSES AS A YOUNG MAN

As Prince-Regent, Ramses was involved in several projects jointly with his father. One was gold mining. Seti knew that within the most eastern part of the desert of Edfu was gold of great value. However, Edfu was notorious for its inhospitality to travelers. It was a land of little water, much sun, and many inhospitable creatures. Seti traveled into the desert approximately forty miles before he became discouraged. His words were even recorded: "How tiresome is this dusty road! How can a man go on plagued by thirst?"

Seti undertook the digging of a well for his future miners. According to later accounts, he found a spring of water which produced little, if anything. Seti put the best face on the project and proclaimed his well a success. This was to have at least one effect on Ramses — he was to retrace these steps and try again.

Ramses also went out in search of granite for his father's statues. He discovered several good sites in the mountains and put them into operation. Statues were built on the sites under Ramses' inspection. They were then transported to their intended place of display. Ramses publicly declared a special affinity for sculptors, stating on an official temple engraving that he would feed them in even the worst famine as well as in prosperity. Throughout his life he would commission innumerable statues of all shapes and sizes. His own likenesses were very flattering and gentle, perhaps because his sculptors appreciated his patronage.

During this period Ramses also learned from his father the great skill of designing temples. Seti was a master builder whose temples were laid out on a scale far grander than any in his own recent history. During this apprenticeship, Ramses began to construct a junior temple at Abydos while his father was working on a major one. His was dedicated to Osiris, as was his father's. However, the workmanship shows an inexperienced hand. Ramses' temple was on a smaller scale and was made more crudely. The carvings were of inferior quality, as if completed too hurriedly.

During this time Ramses also helped oversee construction of Seti's memorial temple on the west bank of the Nile in Thebes. He probably supervised the building of his father's tomb and commissioned his own.

Chapter 7

RECEIVING THE CROWN

Ramses' tenure as Prince-Regent ended suddenly when Seti died at the relatively young age of fifty. Ramses was left to bury his father, to chart the course of his people and to carve his own place in history.

Ramses was only around twenty-five when Seti died. However, he quickly and easily assumed the throne. There was a great tradition of continuity in Egyptian religion which provided the basis for the succession of father to son. To the Egyptians death was simply a passing to a new life. It was the son's sacred duty to see to this passing, and his every action was to be based on the Horus/Osiris legend. The legend had it that Osiris, originator of civilization in Egypt and the model great king, was murdered by his jealous brother Seth. Seth chopped the body into pieces. When Horus, Osiris' son, fought Seth for the throne, he lost one eye. With the help of the eye, Isis, Osiris' wife, formed Osiris' body into one piece. Osiris came back to life, but only in the netherworld, where he was to forever reign and judge the dead. Horus then succeeded his father on earth.

A crucial part of the story was the burial which Horus gave to his father. This rite ensured that Osiris would be happy in the afterworld, and freed Horus to rule unchallenged on earth. Every pharaoh bore the responsibility of doing the same for his own father. If he failed to do so, he was not considered to be a legitimate heir. If someone else performed the last rites, it was he who could claim the throne for himself. It happened on more than one occasion that the oldest son lost the throne to an usurper because he was away on a diplomatic mission at the time of his father's death, and could not perform the burial as required.

However, Ramses was ready to accept the responsibility of seeing to his father's passage to the new world. There was a traditional period of mourning of seventy days, in which Seti's body was to be mummified and the funeral arrangements made. The burial ritual was elaborate. Embalming and mummification took nearly the full seventy days. The inner organs were removed and packed in jars. Then the body was packed with natron and salt to preserve it. Egyptians believed that the body would soon be used again by its previous owner and should therefore be surrounded by the best that life had to offer — fine food, jewelry, clothing, and personal belongings and momentos. Inside the tombs were placed pictures of friends and relatives bringing gifts to the deceased, so that when no one was left to care for the dead, he would instead draw sustenance from the spiritual offerings.

For a pharaoh the needs were far greater, for he was to rule in the heavens, sailing across the sky with the sun-god Re. His subjects would still be bound to him when they joined him in the afterlife. (Everyone would, in fact, remain as they had been in life; they would simply join the ranks of Osiris. A person who died was not referred to as "the late Ramose," for example, but as "the Osiris Ramose.") Seti's body was to be accompanied by the sturdiest of chariots, the most beautiful of scepters, and the most resplendent of headdresses on the great journey ahead.

Ramses' first job was to announce to Egypt that Seti had died, and then to formally accede to the throne. He succeeded his father in early June in 1290 B.C. As it was the third month of summer in Egypt, it was to be a long and hot journey from the king's summer residence in the north to his tomb in Thebes.

By August Seti's body was ready, and the great funeral flotilla set off down the Nile to deliver him to his tomb. Ramses accompanied the casket and took part in the final ritual of touching his father's eyes and mouth to restore them to life in the next world.

Ramses II receives the double crown of Upper and Lower Egypt from the Gods Thoth and Horus. Abu Simbel.

Chapter 8

THE FESTIVAL OF OPET

When the burial rites were completed, Ramses then took part in the Festival of Opet, in honor of Amun. Amun was the chief god, patron of Thebes, beneficiary of the two great temples of Luxor and Karnak. Up until about a century before Ramses' time, Amun was considered to be the true ruler of Egypt, with the pharaoh serving merely as his chief administrator. However, the pharaohs had come to strain under this yoke. They did not care to be subservient to Amun or to his priests. Akhnaten had reduced Amun's prestige, first by elevating other gods, and then by emphasizing his own personal divinity. It became accepted that the pharaoh stood as an equal among the many gods.

Ramses, too, glorified and deified himself. He, like his predecessors, appointed to the priesthood only men he considered to be loyal. He, too, honored gods other than Amun. However, throughout his life he participated in all of the traditional celebrations for Amun, as well as other gods.

This particular rite, the Festival of Opet, was celebrated in Thebes. Opet had traditionally commanded the personal attendance of the pharaohs, who often journeyed from Memphis specifically to enact their role in the acclamation of Amun. The festival lasted three weeks. It began at the Temple of Karnak, where barques carrying images of Amun and lesser gods set off in procession towards the Nile. The pharaoh, bearing an incense burner, led the procession. Once the party arrived at the river, the pharaoh and the officials created the appearance of rowing the barques, which were actually being towed by rope. Along the way people crowded the streets and the river banks, accompanying the barques with songs, acrobatics, and incense burning. As at most festivals, hawkers of rare foods and other delicacies turned a good profit. A short distance up the Nile the barques were finally brought to the Temple of Luxor, where the pharaoh held court on affairs of state for three weeks while the priests carried out sacred rites in the temple. During this time the Pharaoh was guided by oracles from the chief god. Ramses made his first important appointment, the High Priest of Amun, after he received such a message. When the three week period was over, the festivities resumed for the barques' trip home.

This festival was not unusual for Egypt. Torchlight processions, food and drink, story-telling and dancing were common in many local and national celebrations. Throughout these events there was a strong religious flavor, with songs of praise and prayer for the well-being of the pharaoh as the son and servant of the gods.

When the festival was complete Ramses returned to his summer home. This was the site from which his family had originally come, located in northern Egypt near the Mediterranean Sea. He had decided upon his father's death to proclaim it to be a new capital city, even though it was removed from the traditional centers of politics and religion. He named his new city Pi-Ramses, or "home of Ramses of the great victories." At one stroke he established a spot removed from the priesthood of Amun in Thebes, as well as creating a retreat in which his armies could train without threat of attack from outside. Here he was to build an impressive center of state.

Part of the Avenue of Sphinxes at the Temple of Karnak, set up by Ramses II.

Chapter 9

PI-RAMSES

Little remains of Pi-Ramses, but it was a stunning palace according to all descriptions of the time. The many texts refer unceasingly to the delightfully charming atmosphere of the palace, its airy rooms and the sense of wonder and awe it instilled. It is described as having elegant balconies and grandiose halls studded with gems and painted in bright colors.

Pi-Ramses was also a museum of sorts in its own time, preserving and displaying the life of the king. Four colossi stood sixty feet high in its chambers along with a number of finely modelled smaller statues. Depictions of Ramses' childhood and of his filial ties to the gods graced the walls.

At Pi-Ramses, Ramses was most accessible. His court was open to all petitioners and feasts were almost continuous. It was a scene of state ceremony and festive entertainment for most of its residents. However, its location near Canaan was to have a tragic impact on the children of Israel.

Courtyard of the Temple of Seti I at Abydos

Chapter 10

EVERYDAY LIFE FOR RAMSES

Inside the newly emerging Pi-Ramses, Ramses and his family lived a life similar to most wealthy Egyptians. Like other nobility, Ramses had household servants. One personal attendant carried matting on which the Pharaoh stood when he was conversing. Another carried his sandals, which he wore only when he was not walking. Still another, the cupbearer, waited on Ramses' table and supervised meals. This position was a powerful one, for it gave its bearer the opportunity to talk casually with the king and to act as an appointment secretary of sorts.

Egyptians were fastidiously clean. They normally washed when they first woke up and after each meal. To stay fresh during hot weather they covered their bodies with a lotion made with turpentine and incense. Ramses spent hours in the manicurist's chair as well as with his barber. Unlike most men of the time, his hair was cut short so that he could easily change his head-gear.

Ramses ate breakfast alone, typically starting the day with bread, meat, cake and beer. The two later meals he shared with Nefertari, the two of them sitting at a small table, with the children sitting on cushions on the floor nearby. Ramses was awake at dawn, so the family usually retired shortly after their evening meal.

The Egyptians had fifteen different words for bread and cake, and ate both in enormous quantities. Their national drink was beer, sometimes made from dates rather than malt. Egyptians in general were great meat eaters, especially of beef. There was no chicken, but birds and fish were popular. The Egyptians consumed garlic, vegetables and lettuce, which was believed to be an aphrodisiac.

Pi-Ramses was a site of continual luncheons, banquets, and other parties. These occasions called for gold and silver cups, painted pottery and alabaster tableware. Banquets were almost always preceded by lengthy toasts, mainly to the pharaoh and his family. After these preliminaries, men and women were seated on opposite sides of the room, and the meal began. There was always music — often ensembles of harps, zithers, and flutes — and sometimes acrobats or dancers.

Although there was not much time for recreation, Ramses had been brought up accustomed to physical exertion. He was renowned for his strength, endurance, and physical skill. He was an expert archer (as apparently all Egyptians claimed to be) and an excellent horseman. Many pharaohs hunted elephant, lions and wild bulls along the Euphrates, although we have no record of Ramses doing so.

Ramses also took part in the gentler pastimes of hearth and home. An inscription of the time depicts

Nefertari playing Senet, a table game like chess. Ramses' family also had pets. Queen Tuya had a cat, a monkey, and a goose, all of which were allowed to roam the household freely.

Entrance to the Temple of Karnak showing part of the Avenue of Sphinxes and the first pylon of the temple.

Chapter 11

THE FIRST YEARS
AS PHARAOH

Every pharaoh was expected to serve the gods well in order to bring prosperity to his people. One of the most important tasks he would undertake was the building and maintenance of the temples where religious rites were held. Inside these temples priests offered daily meals to the gods, reenacted the burial and resurrection of Osiris, or simply curried the gods' favor.

Temples generally followed a typical construction plan — first the entranceway leading to a courtyard, then an entry hall leading to inner rooms. Deep within was the inner sanctum, where the spirits of the gods were actually present. The pharaoh could demonstrate his close kinship to the gods by placing his own image among theirs, in the form of either a statue or a wall inscription.

Seti had built temples and decorated them on a scale unmatched in generations, and he and Ramses had jointly undertaken several building projects while Ramses was still a youth. In his first years of rule Ramses continued the work of building temples, statues, and memorials. He was mostly occupied with completing and expanding upon work which other pharaohs, .and especially his father, had begun.

THE TEMPLE OF ABYDOS

The Temple of Abydos stood in the city of the same name, the city most sacred to Osiris. Abydos was even in Ramses' time an ancient holy city with much the same significance that Jerusalem has today. Several historical sites were located nearby. A statuette of Cheops, builder of the Great Pyramid at Giza, was housed in a sanctuary only a ten-minute walk from the temple. An ancient adobe fortress lay just to the west.

Many pharaohs had constructed temples or simply their tombs on this site. Although looting had caused the newer dynasties to locate their tombs in the secret Valley of the Kings, there were still religious and symbolic reasons for most Egyptians to maintain some form of tie to the site of Abydos at their death. Osiris was the god of resurrection, and many wished to be buried as close to his resting place as possible. If a nearby burial could not be arranged, the next best thing was to arrange for one's body to be carried on a pilgrimage there before burial. Next best was to set up a memorial stone in Abydos with one's name on it. And if this, too, was impossible, relatives would usually add worship pots (inscribed with the deceased's name) to the enormous mass of similar pots accumulating around the royal tombs.

It was on this site that Seti built what is considered to be his greatest work — a temple of white limestone, decorated with brightly colored scenes. Its coffers were filled with gold. The design was innovative — two entry courts, two halls of columns, and seven sanctuaries for the gods. This was a departure from the standard temple layout, possibly because of a change in religious doctrine, possibly because of the instability of the ground at the site. Seti made his shrines more accessible than usual by including entrances from the outside. Up until then, all shrines had been buried deep within the temple behind an ever-shrinking series of halls.

To Ramses and Seti, the exact structure of the temple was an integral part of its meaning. The loftier and more awe-inspiring the design, the greater was the pharaoh. Every part of the building held a meaning. When Ramses later blocked the outside entrances to five of the sanctuaries, it was probably to symbolize a religious belief in the sanctity of the gods.

Much of the work on this temple was completed in Seti's later years. However, some work remained to be done at the time of his death, and Ramses visited the temple at Abydos shortly after Seti died. He was shocked by the state of disrepair of the cemetery and tombs of past kings. Descendants of the kings had abandoned construction of the tombs at the moment of their fathers' deaths, leaving statues lying in the dust, pillars on their sides, and monuments half-built.

Ramses had been preoccupied with other work, but now he assigned a large complement of workers to restore what had been ruined and to complete his father's temple. He renewed worship services, which had fallen off, ordered new statues carved, and formalized the administration of the temple's revenue-producing lands.

Ramses also began his own temple at Abydos. It is considered to be perhaps the most beautiful of those he initiated himself. The walls were of fine-grained limestone. The pillars were made of sandstone, the door frames of red, black, and gray granite, and the shrine of alabaster. The engravings were of mixed quality. Ramses also included an extensive list of the kings preceding him, perhaps to establish the continuity of the throne.

THE TEMPLE OF KARNAK

Karnak consists of several temples built over a period of 800 years, covering the period before Ramses through the period just before Christ. During this time Karnak was considered to be the national shrine of Egypt. The most important of the temples was the temple of Amun-Re, which is still the largest religious shrine not only in Egypt but in the world. This single temple covered approximately 200 acres in all.

This site, too, called for Ramses' attention, for its majesty and scale established the authority of whomever might call it his. When he ascended to the throne, Ramses' predecessors had already established Karnak as the religious center of the nation. The temples were historical monuments comparable to Rome's Sistine Chapel. Ramses' father, Seti, and grandfather, Ramses I, made their mark on the main building — they filled in the courtyard in front of the Great Temple with a huge hall of columns in honor of Amun. The effect of their addition was well-calculated. The contrast between the sunny entry way to the temple and the darkness of the enclosed hall of columns enhanced the mystery of the temple and induced awe in those who entered.

40

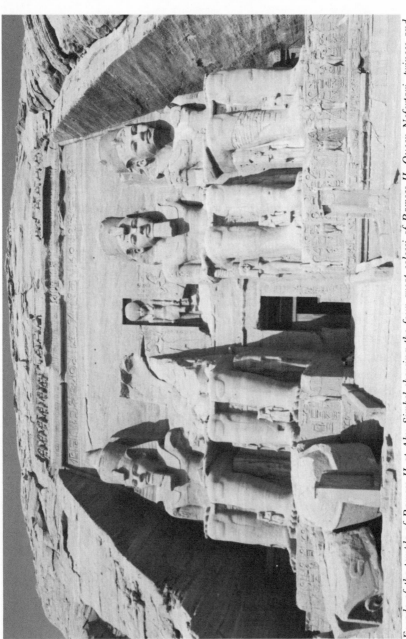

Facade of the temple of Ramses II at Abu Simbel showing the four great colossi of Ramses II. Queen Nefertari, princes and princesses stand between his legs. Re-Horakhti, the sky-god, to whom the temple is dedicated, stands above the doorway.

Ramses continued work on the hall during his early years as pharaoh and completed it in approximately the forty-fifth year of his reign. This hall has become one of the Great Wonders of the Ancient World. When Ramses had finally finished the hall, it covered approximately 54,000 square feet and contained 134 columns. The largest twelve columns measured 69 feet high, 11 3/4 feet in diameter, and more than 33 feet in circumference. The columns were built of reddish-brown sandstone semi-drums, which were sculpted separately and then assembled in the temple. Each of the open flower capitals left today has room on top for about 100 people to stand.

Seti carved a vast battle relief upon the interior of the hall depicting his military victories in Canaan, Syria, and Libya. These reliefs were delicately cut in low relief and many were painted with beautiful colors. Ramses appropriated credit for his father's work by renaming the room, "Effective is Ramses II." Later, Ramses added reliefs of himself being blessed by the gods. Ramses' workmanship was not as fine as that of his father. His inscriptions were crudely and deeply cut.

Ramses' reliefs are typical in their portrayal of the pharaoh's closeness to the gods of the Egyptian pantheon. In one relief, he makes an offering to the god Amun, offering him emblems of the renewal festivals. Amun then grants Ramses the symbol of many festivals, indicating a long life and a long reign. Ramses also makes an offering to his father Seti, who now rules with the gods in the Netherworld. The importance of unity between Upper and Lower Egypt is underscored by the relief which shows Ramses kneeling on the emblem of union.

He is bordered on one side by a lotus (the symbol for Lower Egypt) and on the other side by papyrus (the symbol for Upper Egypt) while the two gods Horus and Thot tie the knot of unity.

Ramses later used the walls of this temple to recount the battle he would fight at Kadesh — once in the Hall of Columns and once again on the southern approach to the temple. Still later he recorded the great Hittite peace treaty on a wall nearby.

Ramses was not content to leave the temple in its natural setting along the river. A paved boat landing had been built to measure the flooding of the Nile. Ramses lined the avenue from the quay to the temple with sphinxes bearing rams' heads. The sphinxes have since been moved into the temple grounds, where they now watch over the entrance to the ruins of the temple.

At Karnak Ramses also built two colossal granite statues of himself, which he placed within the temple grounds. On each figure a smaller figurine of Nefertari stood in front of him, her head reaching just above his knees. Later (at the Temples of Abu Simbel) she was to stand as his equal.

THE LUXOR TEMPLE

Nearby, also in Thebes, was the ancient Temple of Luxor. It, too, was impressive in appearance, its colonnades visible to all travelers along the Nile. It covered four acres in all.

The work on the temple of Luxor was the first which Ramses completed, sometime during the third year of his reign. In this temple Ramses constructed a new forecourt, with obelisks and huge colossi of himself covering the south wall. Tossing modesty aside, he placed huge granite figures of himself on the throne on either side of the entrance.

Ramses was particularly proud of the research he had done on the history of the temple in the "House of Life," Luxor's archive of religious mysteries. His inscriptions in the temple show detailed knowledge of the myths surrounding Re, with whom he had announced a special and favored relationship. He refers to Thebes as the "Eye of Re" and as the original site of the origin of the earth. In one inscription he appeals to the sense of unity in Egypt by using the god Amun's right eye to represent the south, and his left, the north. One cannot work without the other.

THE TEMPLES OF ABU SIMBEL

Abu Simbel was, among other things, Ramses' tribute to Nefertari. He began work on the temples when he was between thirty and thirty-five years old. He chose to build not one temple there, but two — one for himself and a second one jointly dedicated to Nefertari and to the local goddess Hathor.

Nefertari had been at Ramses' side from the beginning of his reign. She had gone with him to Thebes during his first year as Pharaoh, sharing in the funeral rites for his father. When the Luxor temple additions were completed in the third year of Ramses' tenure, she appeared prominently in the engravings, and her figure was carved on the colossal statues that Ramses built for the temple's interiors. In practically every family scene, it was Nefertari who appeared with her mother-in-law and the children. Ramses' temples at Abu Simbel demonstrated what a large role she had come to play in his life.

Abu Simbel's two magnificent sand and stone temples were carved into the cliffs overlooking the waters of the Nile in Nubia to the south. Ramses did not pick the site merely because of the existence of suitable rock faces. The site symbolized Egypt's strong political and economic presence in the southern province of Nubia. In addition, this area had been considered sacred for at least five centuries before Ramses became Pharaoh. Ramses was choosing a location for his fabulous undertaking which would inspire awe and reverence everywhere.

Everything about Ramses' own Great Temple was and is colossal. Carved out of solid rock, it is one hundred and eight feet high, one hundred twenty-four feet wide, and is embedded more than two hundred feet deep into the mountain. Thousands of years later, the temple is still visually stunning. The facade is a huge pylon on which are carved four colossi of the king, two on each side of the entrance. Their shoulders measure twenty-five feet across. Ramses is shown at his prime, not as the young man depicted in engravings at Abydos or Karnak. Around and between the legs of his colossi are grouped, as was the custom, members of the royal family — wives, parents, and children. Nefertari appears three times.

On the sides of the thrones of the two middle colossi are depictions of the Nile gods binding the symbolic plants of Upper and Lower Egypt around the "Sma." The sma (a windpipe with lungs) was a symbol of the unity of Upper and Lower Egypt. Above this scene stands Ramses, and below are slaves from the north and south.

Within the temple there are numerous thirty-foot high figures of Ramses supporting a ceiling decorated with flying vultures and stars. The reliefs on the walls consist of battle scenes and family scenes from Ramses' life.

The inner sanctuary is especially impressive. The recessed area in the rear wall holds the seated figures of four gods — Ptah, Amun, Ramses II, and Harakhti. During solstices (around February 23 and October 23) the rays of the rising sun strike these figures just at dawn. The axis of the temple was laid perfectly so that the sunlight would illuminate the group of gods two hundred feet within the heart of the cliff.

Just north of the Great Temple was built the temple of Queen Nefertari. Today the two temples are separated from each other by a ravine in which a permanent flood of sand flows. However, there was no rift between king and queen in Ramses' day.

Nefertari's temple is not as large as Ramses'. The width of the facade is only ninety-two feet and its height thirty-nine feet. However, the workmanship is excellent and has an intimacy and femininity that indicates the respect that Ramses had for his wife. On either side of the entrance there are three figures. Each grouping contains two statues of Ramses with Nefertari in the center. One inscription reads "This temple was made as an eternal work in the land of Nubia," another, "Nothing like this has been made before." Still another says, "For

Facade of the Temple of Queen Nefertari at Abu Simbel showing two colossal statues of Ramses II. Below a row of sacred cobras guarding the doorway, Ramses II offers wine to Amun-Re and Horus.

Nefertari, for whom the very sun does shine." On the inner walls of the temple, the king and queen stand united before the gods. Only in the inner sanctuary does Ramses play the dominating role. He is snuggled under Hathor, who appears as the figure of a protective mother cow over her son.

(The temples of Abu Simbel were imperiled in the 1960's by the construction of the Aswan Dam. With international support, they were dismantled, stone by stone, and re-erected two hundred feet higher on the cliff. During the salvage operation, the temples were sawed into blocks, twenty to thirty tons each, and reassembled above, much as the ancient Egyptians themselves constructed their colossal statuary.)

OTHER PROJECTS

During this time Ramses decided to once again tackle the problem of mining for gold in the desert. Upon the advice of his aides, he tried to establish a well for prospective workers. He consulted with his advisors to find the proper location for the well, and the record shows that they assured him that he had the power to establish a well wherever he pleased. He needed only to call upon his godly powers. Fortunately, Ramses succeeded where his father had failed. He struck water only eighteen feet below the surface. Mining began shortly afterward.

After this experience, Ramses turned his attention to the glories of Egypt as a conqueror nation. Despite her somewhat diminished status, Egypt was still the greatest power in the region. Each year her soldiers patrolled the streets of numerous tribute-paying states, and she had the might to prevent pirates from readily approaching her port cities. Her army stood ready and able to quell any rebellion. Each summer Ramses set out on a military campaign to either protect some threatened stronghold or to increase Egypt's holdings.

In his fourth year, without warning, Ramses marched on Syria, where he had been with his father a decade earlier. He caught the local inhabitants by surprise, but fell short of taking Kadesh, the regional capital. However, he completely forced the controlling Hittites out of the region and felt confident of taking the city the next year. He was unaware that on the other side of Syria, the Hittites were assembling allies from sixteen other provinces to recapture the territory. The stage was thus set for the battle which was to be one of the major events of Ramses' life.

Ramses II in his chariot at the Battle of Kadesh. Temple of Ramses II at Abu Simbel.

Chapter 12

THE BATTLE OF KADESH

In his fifth year Ramses decided that the time was right to drive the Hittites from northern Syria. Ramses picked the end of April to begin his effort. He planned to strike first at Kadesh, the city both he and his father had unsuccessfully tried to recapture for Egypt.

The plan was for Ramses to lead the main body of men overland to Kadesh and there to meet a cadre of supporting troops who would take a sea route. He divided his army into four divisions, called Amun, Re, Ptah, and Seth, after the four gods whose power he wished to invoke (as was customary). He was accompanied by at least two of his sons, as well as their cousins and other relatives.

The army reached Kadesh after one month's march. They camped south of the city the first night and set out early in the morning to find a spot from which they could attack.

Ramses' royal party was far ahead of the main body of the army, which stretched for several miles behind the warrior-king. As Ramses approached a stream outside the city limits, two nomads of the nearby desert approached him and offered to bring their tribesmen into Ramses' camp in his battle against the Hittites. Ramses asked where these tribes were, and the two replied that they were with the Hittites who were one hundred and twenty miles to the north. They said that the Hittite chief, Muwatallis, had retreated when he had heard of the pharaoh's approach.

Ramses was delighted with this news. He felt he had been blessed by the gods — an easy trip out of Egypt, an easy victory at Kadesh to inspire his men, and then on to victory in the north. He selected a site just outside of town to set up camp for the next day's siege.

As camp was being assembled, Ramses sent out a reconnaissance party, who stumbled upon two Hittite spies. After an intense interrogation, these spies revealed that the Hittites were not one hundred and twenty miles away, but rather were just on the other side of Kadesh, ready to strike. Ramses called his generals together, but it was too late. The Hittites had begun their attack.

The Egyptians were totally unprepared. One division, Re, was still crossing the small stream which flowed outside the city limits. The others were far behind. Ramses sent out a desperate call for the troops in the rear to come forward, and sent his sons and their young relatives to the west, safely away from the battle.

The Hittites cut through the befuddled Re division and fell upon what was assembled of Ramses' camp. The soldiers in the camp panicked when they saw the Re division in retreat with the Hittites in hot pursuit. They broke what rank existed and scattered to save their own lives. Ramses and his immediate entourage were left unprotected, with only their armour and shields, and their skills as archers.

Ramses attempted first to rally his troops, but was ignored in the panic. Perhaps it was his training, perhaps it was his faith that the gods were with him, perhaps it was his desire to live up to his father's reputation — whatever propelled him, he boldly drove a course that could only be described as heroic. He gathered the few men near him and charged again and again into the center of the battle. He repelled the Hittites around him and created the semblance of a true resistance being put up by the Egyptians.

Ramses' bold actions saved his own life and helped to delay the overrun of the camp long enough for the unexpected arrival of the supporting troops who had agreed to meet Ramses at this spot. The supporting troops attacked the Hittites from the rear. Fearing that they might be trapped between the two armies, the Hittites drew back. This movement allowed the Egyptians to rally and renew their attack. Ramses led the charge again and again, forcing the Hittites to pull back further and further.

Muwatallis, on the other side of the city, did not realize what was going on. Thinking that an easy victory was assured, he had reserved a large number of his men from battle. It was already too late when he realized that the Egyptians had miraculously turned the tide.

Both sides remained in camp that night. Ramses had only two divisions in fighting shape, Ptah and Seth, in addition to the supporting troops. The Hittites numbered twice as many. However, Muwatallis had lost two of his brothers and many of his personal entourage in the battle. Neither side was well prepared for further battle.

Ramses decided to attack the next morning, perhaps thinking that surprise could help him overcome the disparity in the size of the two armies. The Hittites managed to hold their own, but they were too weak to dislodge the Egyptians, and the two sides settled in for what looked like a drawn-out struggle of endurance.

Muwatallis was the first to decide that perhaps the best way out was to resort to diplomacy. He sent a proposal to Ramses, suggesting that a ceasefire be called and that both sides withdraw. Ramses consulted his advisors and they encouraged him to accept. He conceded to a ceasefire, but would not agree to sign a treaty with Muwatallis. He obviously had intentions to come back and try again, perhaps because of injured pride or a desire to do what his father had not been able to.

Ramses was profoundly affected by what had happened. He did not regard it as just another battle. He was to tell this story again and again. He commissioned two written versions of the story, one prose and one poetry. He inscribed the tale on the walls of every major temple he had constructed and would construct — Abydos, Karnak, Luxor, and Abu Simbel, and his own personal memorial temple, the Ramesseum.

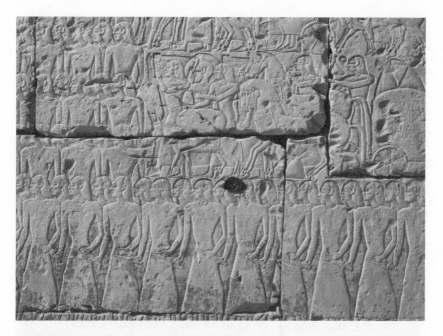

Battle scenes of the Battle of Kadesh on the river Orontes in Syria. Temple of Ramses II, Abydos.

The poetic version of the encounter is the oldest known example of the narrative battle poem, which would later become a standard form of literature. The poem particularly exaggerates Ramses' role in the battle and omits the part of the story in which Ramses is deceived by the nomadic tribesmen. It is very religious in nature. The description of the pharaoh's plight includes an appeal to Amun which is similar to the prayers of any soldier in battle:

> No one, including my charioteer, my soldier, and my shieldbearer, stood by my side as I faced the enemy. I spoke to Amun, crying "What is happening, Father? Can you justly ignore your son? Am I so insignificant? Don't I take my every step at your command? I have not failed to do anything you have asked. You are too great, Lord of Egypt, to allow heathens to trample you! What significance can they have to you? Haven't I fulfilled my obligations — built you monuments, filled your coffers with gold, built for you an eternal home, given you everything I own? I have given you land to support your rites, I have sacrificed ten thousand cattle for you and every form of spice and herb. I have never drawn back from doing what is right in meeting the demands of justice. I have built great temples and personally seen to the smallest details. I brought you Obelisks from Yebu and carried the stones myself. I dedicated my ships to feeding you. Do you want men to say that there is little to be gained from trusting in you? Help me, the man who relies on

your aid, the man who serves you wholeheart-
edly. I am calling you, surrounded here by
people I don't know, surrounded by enemies.
No one is standing by me, I am alone. My
men have left me here, not one searches me
out. But I know that you can help me more
than a million troops or thousands of
charioteers, more than hundreds of the most
devoted brothers. You are stronger than any
nation. I am here because you placed me
here. I have done nothing wrong."

Ramses was not to forget the panic of his troops
nor the loyalty of the men immediately around him. A
large portion of the poem is a harangue against the men
who failed him:

I shouted to my men, "Courage! See how I
alone am able to win a victory, for Amun is
at my side. Why are you so full of fear —
none of you is faithful to me. Haven't I done
enough for you? Didn't I raise you to honor
in my ranks? I have watched over the son as
well as the father, and I have driven out evil
from our land. I have given you servants,
returned what you have lost. When you asked
for a favor, I always replied, let it be done.
No nobleman has done more for his men
than I have. I haven't pressed you into constant battle. I have allowed you to live with
your families and trusted that you would be
true to me in war as in peace. But you have
all acted like cowards — not one of you stood
your ground, not one came to my aid. As

Amun lives, I wish that I had not witnessed this travesty, that I had never undertaken to challenge the Hittites. None of you can claim that you served your country. What a repayment for my work erecting temples in Thebes! Words can't express the disgrace you have brought upon yourselves!"

When Menena, my shieldbearer saw that I was surrounded, he began to tremble with fear. He said to me, "Great Pharaoh of Egypt, we have been abandoned by the others in the thick of battle — why are you trying to defend them? Let us escape!" I said, "Stand firm! I will attack as a falcon, slaying without mercy. Why are you afraid of such a miserable lot?" I then plunged into the masses with as much force as I could, again and again. I was like a god, killing unceasingly.

I said to my men "How shall I deal with you now that you have shown yourselves un-trustworthy? Haven't you come here to attain honor, to return home with my commendation? A man who fights bravely in war is honored for the rest of his life. Haven't I treated you well enough to deserve your bravery in battle? You're fortunate that you survived the attack, since you did nothing to repel the enemy as I stood alone. Don't you know deep down that I am your shield? What will your countrymen say when they hear that you abandoned me with no one, not the low-liest of defenders to stand with me? Look who was there when I was alone, my two horses! They were with me as I fought the foreigners! I will personally feed them every day when we have returned to my palace. It was my horses whom I found at my side — and my charioteer, my shieldbearer and my cupbearers. They have witnessed my role in battle. Them I found."

Ramses also described the next day's events, adding some luster to the conclusion of the campaign:

At dawn I prepared to attack, eager to carry on the battle. I dedicated my efforts to the gods, ready for victory. I was as relentless as a falcon or a serpent hissing. I was like the early burst of the sun at dawn, my rays scorching the enemy. They said to each other, "Don't fight this man — the great goddess Sekhmet is on his side, guiding his steps, leading his horses. Anyone who dares to challenge him will be burned as by fire!" And so they kept their distance, bowing to the ground. My majesty overwhelmed them and I left them sprawling before my horses, lying in their own blood.

Ramses was to boast of his courage for the rest of his life. Perhaps his proven strength later allowed him to act as a conciliator when it became appropriate.

The time for conciliation was not at hand, however. Ramses returned to Egypt without his final victory, but with undiminished enthusiasm for the task of regaining

Egyptian control of Syria. He rebuilt his army and prepared for continued war. He was not disappointed, but the threat did not come from Syria. Several nearby provinces, having seen Ramses' army retreating, ended their payment of tributes. Ramses mustered his men and quickly put down the rebellion.

Over the next few years Ramses continued his attack on Syria. He won battle after battle. However, his successes were never final, for the territories he defeated kept re-aligning with the Hittites as soon as he left. Perhaps it was a recognition of the futility of his efforts that caused Ramses to spend less and less time attacking his Hittite neighbors. In any event, Ramses began devoting more time to construction than to the military.

Chapter 13

THE EXODUS

Foreigners had made their homes in Egypt for centuries. In particular, Semitic speaking peoples had been granted land in northern Egypt by Hyksos invaders just two centuries before Ramses. East of Pi-Ramses, Ramses' hometown and new urban center, was Goshen. For years nomads had grazed sheep in this area without interference. However, Ramses, used to having forced labor at his command, saw the opportunity to press these people into the job of constructing his new city. He needed a supply of unskilled labor to finish the undertaking. He was nearing forty and could not know how long he would live — only fifteen years if he had inherited his father's life span.

Ramses first took a census of the people, then pressed them into lugging stones and making bricks. In the Bible the book of Exodus specifically identifies Ramses as the oppressor of the children of Israel. Exodus 1:12-14 describes how the Egyptians felt they must drive the laborers in order to keep them under control: "But the more they afflicted them, the more they multiplied and grew and they were in dread of the children of Israel. So the

Egyptians made the children of Israel serve with rigor and they made their lives bitter with hard bondage — in mortar, in brick and in all manner of service in the field."

Ramses thought of forced laborers as tools rather than as humans, despite his kindness toward his own Egyptian laborers. Perhaps he had become immune to the tragedy of slavery because of his early exposure to the taking of captives in battle.

No one is sure whether or not Ramses is the pharaoh of the Exodus. It has been speculated that it was one of Ramses' youngest daughters, Meri, who found Moses in the bulrushes. Some estimates place the Exodus in the first half of Ramses' tenure, when he was about forty. There are no Egyptian accounts of the event, but that is not surprising. Egyptian scribes and storytellers were not particularly fond of recording plagues, ruined crops, or the loss of a contingent of forced labor.

If Ramses was indeed the pharaoh of the Exodus, we have been provided with a glimpse of a very stubborn nature. Ramses' unwillingness to sign a treaty in Kadesh and his return to the gold mines after his father's failure confirm this. By all accounts, Ramses did not like to give up.

Ramses certainly was not able to see any justness in the Israelites' cause. Egyptians were tolerant of other countries' gods, and even adopted some. They were even more accepting of the multitude of gods within Egypt itself. Each locality had its own special gods and every town had its own sacred tree. However, Egyptians saw nothing in an argument for one god, especially the god of what they believed to be of inferior people.

This is not to say that Egyptians were non-religious. On the contrary, religious beliefs pervaded their lives. Herodutus considered them to be the most painstakingly religious of all cultures. Much of their literature was concerned with the principles of a righteous life.

Egyptian religious doctrine is still an enigma to us. Varying interpretations have been put forth for the role of the eye, and the six sacred parts of the body, as well as for the meaning of the gods and their incarnations as falcons, crocodiles, bulls, or birds. Despite the differences, however, there is agreement that the Egyptians were a pious and moralistic people.

Ramses, as all other Egyptians, saw all of the gods as personal gods who were capable of responding to prayer. He attributed his success at Kadesh to Amun's intervention. When he established Pi-Ramses, he apparently did not want to leave out any important gods, and assembled a huge collection of images, including those of neighboring Syria and Phoenicia.

Ramses took the construction and maintenance of temples very seriously, and spared no expense. He believed that the gods within spoke to him, often through eye movements or small signals. If a statue nodded its head or leaned toward an official at the appropriate moment, it was taken as a sign of favor or assent to the question at hand.

Commoners, too, sought the assistance of the gods. The dieties were, like the Hebrews' god, considered to be great levellers and restorers of justice. Anyone could come to the temple at the appointed time and enter into a conversation with a god concerning even the most mundane problem. The gods were sympathetic toward the poor, and would help a man even when all other men had turned against him. Since the poor were often victims of official corruption, overbearing public servants, and high taxes, this promise of justice was not unappreciated.

Even the poorest man hoped for a better life in the afterworld. Graves discovered today inevitably contain items a living person would find useful and comforting; toys for children, food and clothing for adults. Egyptians believed they would be judged at death, and in their burial sites they often included lists of their good deeds as well as lists of sins they had avoided. A typical list would include several statements: "I gave generously to the poor. I respected my parents. I was faithful to my wife. I have not caused anyone to suffer. I have not lied or robbed." This negative confession was an integral part of judgment after death. Many surviving lists are very refined, including small items such as talking too loudly in front of an employer.

Although the gods were sympathetic to the poor, it was the wealthy who contributed the finest jewels and stones, and the finest gold decorations, to the temples. Storehouses in the temples held some of the most extravagant shows of wealth in history. And yet temples were not merely places of worship and offering, but also housed schools for scribes, draftsmen, engineers, and sculptors. They also held the archives and libraries containing not only sacred scripts and texts, but books on ethics and practical advice for living. Religion was an integral part of the daily routine which occupied rich and poor alike.

Ramses' attitude toward the Hebrews, then, must have been that they were far from being a chosen people, and certainly not a threat to his close relationship to the gods. He might have laughed to learn that centuries later when one of his first colossi was discovered by western civilization, it would be wrongly identified as Moses.

Bound african captives taken by Ramses II positioned under his feet at the entrance to the Temple of Ramses II at Abu Simbel.

Chapter 14

HITTITE PEACE

While Ramses may have been brutal in his treatment of other cultures, he had respect for the military capabilities of the Hittites. He had skirmished with them on many occasions over the years, with no conclusive results. Each summer's victory was followed by a setback of one sort or another. Ramses was past the age of forty and had failed to extend the Egyptian domain in any significant way.

The issue came to a head when internal Hittite politics took an unusual turn. The Hittite king, Urhi-Teshud, was trying to keep his uncle Hattusil from achieving too much power. He kept encroaching upon Hattusil's territory, removing more and more land from his uncle's control. He finally attempted to take over the one city in which Hattusil was the local favorite as well as the high priest, and this proved to be one city too many. Hattusil attacked and captured the young king and sent him into exile in northern Syria.

Urhi-Teshub decided to approach Ramses for protection. To Hattusil this was an immense threat, for an alliance of Egypt with his nephew was likely to overwhelm him. Shortly afterward, Hattusil approached Ramses and suggested that they sign a pact of friendship. Ramses, depite his earlier stubbornness and perhaps because he was tired of wars which brought so little glory, agreed.

The treaty was not unlike any modern alliance. Both parties agreed to refrain from attacking one another, as well as to defend each other from attacks by common enemies. They agreed to mutually extradite fugitives as long as the fugitives would be treated humanely. (The one exception was Urhi, who lived in Egypt for at least ten years after the pact was signed.) One section of the pact provided that each king would fight to ensure that the other's plan of succession was put into effect, promising that Hattusil's and Ramses' sons would reign after them. As usual for any state affair, the gods were called upon to bless the undertaking.

Ramses was enthusiastic about the pact at the beginning. He made it an occasion for official festivities, and sent presents and official proclamations of friendship to the Hittites. To demonstrate Hittite cordiality, Hattusil's wife sent a letter to Nefertari. Not to be outdone, Nefertari and Tuya sent presents of jewelry and the finest Egyptian royal clothing to their Hittite counterparts.

The treaty did not ensure that the Egyptian-Hittite friendship would be without problems. It wasn't long before troubles began. Ramses was skilled as a warrior, but not as a diplomat. His demeanor was demanding and overbearing. After some official correspondence Hattusil protested that he was being treated like a subject rather than an equal. Ramses could have easily entered into a quarrel that would have broken the treaty. Instead, he wisely used restraint and sent a message praising Hattusil in very diplomatic terms. The breach was healed. Soon afterwards, Ramses sent Egyptian doctors to consult with the Hittites, thus earning a reputation as a valuable and trustworthy ally.

This colossal statue in the forecourt of the Temple of Karnak may represent Ramses II with his wife, Queen Nefertari standing between his knees.

Chapter 15

RAMSES ALONE

It was not long after the treaty was signed that Ramses began to lose the important people in his life. His mother Tuya died when Ramses was about forty-five. He buried her in the Valley of the Queens, where she lay in a pink granite sarcophagus, surrounded by the most elegant of furnishings, deeply mourned by her son.

A few years later, Ramses and Nefertari traveled to Abu Simbel to dedicate the nearly-completed temples there. They timed the visit to see the gods illuminated by the dawn's light in the sanctuary of the Great Temple. Their oldest daughter Meryetamun accompanied them and took part in the rites.

This is the last record of Nefertari accompanying her husband. The record shows that she was already taking a secondary role in the rites. Ramses was escorted by Meryetamun to the altar. Historians believe that Nefertari died shortly thereafter, depriving Ramses of both his mother and his beloved wife in the short period of a few years.

Nefertari's tomb remains today as an example of beauty and elegance. It was the finest in the Valley of the Queens. The walls were built with white stucco, decorated with paintings of the gods and with inscriptions from sacred writings concerning the netherworld. Nefertari is depicted warmly, playing games and being protected on her voyage beyond. As she dies she watches the sun rising between the lions of yesterday and tomorrow.

For a short while, Istnofret, the mother of Ramses' most trusted son, took Nefertari's place. Bint-Anath, Istnofret's oldest daughter and Ramses' oldest child, became a queen at this time, too, symbolically stepping into her mother's role as second consort. Both appeared in inscriptions of the time, but Ramses did not honor either woman as he had Nefertari. No great temple bore their names.

Ramses was to never again find the companionship Nefertari had provided him. After Istnofret's death, Bint-Anath assumed her role as chief consort and even bore Ramses a daughter. Although she outlived Ramses, she did not serve as his queen throughout his life. He took several of her sisters as queens, none lasting, perhaps none serving as more than an official representative at festivals and ceremonies. Ramses buried three of his daughters — Bint-Anath, Meryetamun, and Nebttawy — regally with Nefertari and Istnofret in the Valley of the Queens. However, their images were barely noticeable in the works which Ramses completed during this time.

Chapter 16

HITTITE MARRIAGE

Although he never again formed a strong romantic liason, Ramses did enter into one marriage which was to create a stir in international politics. When Ramses was around fifty-five, Hattusil sent an envoy proposing that the Pharaoh take Hattusil's daughter in marriage. Along with her would come a huge dowry of gold, silver, horses, oxen, goats, and sheep.

Ramses sent back a message of assent, and arranged for his prospective wife to be met by a royal escort under the care of the gods. She came through the land of Canaan with great pomp and ceremony and arrived at Pi-Ramses in the middle of the winter.

Ramses gave her the name "Maat-Neferu-Re" or "the king's wife who sees the beauty of Re." They celebrated a huge wedding at Pi-Ramses and Maat-Neferu-Re was given an honored place in the palace, equal with the princess-queens. The queen's image soon began to appear on amulets, foundation stones, and royal statuary. A year after their marriage, Ramses commissioned a poem declaring the significance of his alliance with the

Hittites. However, by then there was no mention of his love for the queen, and before long she left Pi-Ramses for another palace one hundred and twenty miles away. She was not to replace either Nefertari or the princess-queens.

Five years later, after the relationship between the Hittite chief Hattusil and Ramses had grown quite strong, Hattusil offered Ramses another of his daughters. There was another burst of fanfare, but this marriage had even fewer romantic overtones than did the earlier one. The marriage entered into Egyptian legend — generations of Egyptians were to adopt as a cultural ideal the foreign princess who came to rule as queen in their land. However, the second bride probably followed her sister away from Pi-Ramses soon after the marriage. Ramses was again without a peer at his side.

Chapter 17

RAMSES AS RULER

Throughout this time Ramses was building his reputation as a strong leader. Although at many times in his life he acted stubbornly, vainly and without compassion, he brought a period of well-being to Egypt that was not to be matched for many generations. In his daily administrative duties, he was to show several characteristics that are marks of leadership, among them fairness and loyalty to his people.

The pharaoh in Egypt was not officially responsible for the welfare of his people — the gods were. If the gods were happy, then the Nile would supply its bounteous gifts throughout the year. Therefore, one of Ramses' chief jobs was to appease, praise, and cajole the gods, hoping for their aid. Ramses excelled in constructing temples for the gods, and took part scrupulously in the major religious rites and festivals which tradition dictated he attend. He left his subjects in no doubt that he was attending to their needs.

Ramses personally chose all of the high officials in his administration. One of the most solemn choices was of the High Priest of Amun, which even Ramses was unwilling to make without consulting an oracle. In many of his choices he exhibited a fairness which had escaped other pharaohs.

In ancient Egypt, a man's son usually had first claim on his job when he died or retired to an easier job. It was extremely difficult for any man to rise above his class. Ramses studied the records of men who had served, and although he did not cultivate peasant leaders, he often appointed on merit rather than solely on blood relationships. Although Ramses often touted his own lofty position, he was able to reach down into the ranks to find men of talent.

In this ability he was following the example of his father. Early in his rule Seti had appointed Paser — a man of noble blood but only thirty at the time — as vizier, one of the most responsible positions in the nation. This young man was to prove himself later, but his appointment created a stir at the time. In a culture committed to justice, the Ramsesside dynasty was a popular one.

Chapter 18

A SENSE OF JUSTICE

Egypt was a society of strict rules, which even the pharaoh was expected to obey. Like his predecessors, Ramses followed a daily schedule of waking, reading his mail, bathing and dressing, offering a sacrifice to the gods, and receiving instruction from his priests before taking on a day's work. During the day he held audiences and delivered judgments. Ramses was expected to supervise construction and to visit his holdings up and down the Nile. He was also expected to be knowledgeable, and he invested time in preparing himself for his duties — he visited the archives of the Temple at Abydos on more than one occasion, and was familiar with some of the intricacies of architecture and sculpture.

Ramses' sense of obedience to the rules extended to his justice system. Judges in those times were not perfect — they were often accused of siding with the wealthy, if not actually accepting bribes. However, Seti had set a standard of honesty, threatening to punish officials who stole from the people. Ramses followed this example.

It was in Ramses' reign that one singular law case was finally settled after over a century in the courts. It involved a large piece of land which Pharaoh Ahmose I had given to a man named Neshi for his loyalty. Neshi left the property to all of his descendants in common. The land was not to be divided. The case first came to court when sibling rivalry caused Neshi's children to request that the land be broken up into sections. The court allowed this to be done, but overall control was given to the oldest sister. A second lawsuit asked that the sister's power be taken away. This accomplished, the third lawsuit asked to give the sister her powers back.

This wrangling continued for three generations. In Ramses' early years as Pharaoh, one side of the family bribed an official to give them complete control of the land, expelling a young scribe, Moze, and his family. When Moze was older, he in turn brought suit, charging that the officials had falsified the land records. Near the end of Ramses' reign, the case was finally resolved. Moze was given the land which was rightfully his, and the corrupt official was branded a scoundrel.

Perhaps it is coincidence that the case came to a fair conclusion in Ramses' years, perhaps not. Ramses attempted to clean his administration of corruption. He became personally involved in the case of a storehouse manager who was filching supplies, and promised punishment to any of his administrators who cheated his workers. As his successors learned, this was not an easy job. Years after Ramses' death, teams of looters systematically went their way with little or no interference.

Chapter 19

THE WORKERS' LOT

Ramses developed a reputation for treating his workers, if not his slaves, well. Ramses issued several memorandums commanding that nothing be held back from his men in terms of the necessities of daily life. They were given permission to take time for everything from funerals and religious rites, to brewing beer for upcoming festivals. They were also allowed to devote time to other projects.

Under Ramses' command were state officials, engineers and craftsmen for his construction projects, and the armed forces. But his favored workers were those who built tombs in the Valley of the Kings behind the city of Thebes. These men lived in a village built especially for them, consisting of seventy row-type houses made of mud-brick. For these men the work week was eight days long, with two days off for errands, distribution of supplies, and resting. The work was difficult — digging long corridors into the limestone hills and then constructing tombs for the king deep within. The men were considered to be an elite corps, and Ramses spared no expense in providing them with tools, supplies, and small luxuries.

Ramses' reign was perhaps most beneficial to the peasant. The vast majority of Egyptians were peasants working on the land. Many worked for the temples, which owned approximately one-tenth of the best land in the country. Others worked for large landowners. All had to pay taxes on the little they grew.

Work began at dawn and continued until evening had set in. The tools were primitive. Peasants were always faced with the prospect of a crop lost to locusts or flooding. Ramses often recruited (and possibly forced) peasants to work on his construction projects, which served as a sort of enforced welfare for those of little means.

During Ramses' rule, the peasants were relatively well off. Peasants were often depicted heading toward the marketplace with donkeys loaded high with produce. Most peasants aspired to having a garden, a relative luxury. The small size of the cattle used for plowing indicates that the work was not particularly heavy. Farmers often worked in pairs, further reducing the load.

Ramses did not spare his subjects the burden of taxes. Just before each harvest, Ramses' scribes and surveyors headed for the land to measure the fields and to figure the number of grains per bushel. There were often disputes as to the taxes owed. Tombs of the time often carried the claim, "I did not falsify my grain count," presumably because this was a common practice. Presumably, too, the claimant had enough to live comfortably without cheating the government.

Chapter 20

POMP AND CEREMONY
AT THE ROYAL COURT

One of Ramses' favorite ceremonies was the awarding of medals and gifts to outstanding citizens. This practice had begun long before as a tribute to war heroes but by Ramses' time had been extended to loyal civilians as well. Ramses stood on his balcony while groups of fortunate recipients waited below to receive jewelry, gold, or whatever else the pharaoh was inspired to give. A crowd usually gathered and cheered the goings-on. Both men and women were honored in this way, for anything from extreme bravery to loyal service. The ceremonies were immensely popular.

Ramses' appearance alone was enough to create awe in his followers. His attire was more elaborate by far than even the finest costumes of his military and civilian leaders. He always wore some form of headdress, even in the privacy of his home. During ceremonies he wore a double crown with spirals and tapers of gold projecting from the front and the back. For military occasions he wore a large blue helmet with streamers down the back.

At minimum he wore a decorated wig, with perhaps the flat headpiece used as the base for his crowns. Some of his more elaborate headdresses balanced feathers and horns so delicately that Ramses had to remain motionless throughout the event for which he wore them. Ramses also wore an artificial beard, braided and held to his chin by a strap connected to his crown.

Ramses' jewelry was also remarkable. On state occasions he wore a large beaded necklace and a minimum of three sets of bracelets — one each for his upper arms, wrists, and ankles. He usually appeared in an elegantly buckled belt with a bull's tail hanging behind.

When Nefertari was at Ramses' side, her beauty enhanced rather than diminished her power. Beauty was a huge asset in ancient Egypt, and women used ornaments and makeup extensively from a young age. Nefertari wore broad collar necklaces of gold, carnelian and feldspar — the rich red, blues, and golds were considered to be charms against evil as well as baubles. A headdress weighing four and a half pounds symbolized wealth, prestige and strength. The more elaborate her headdresses and crowns, the more favorable her relationship to the gods.

The height of ceremonial attire was saved for the reception of foreign diplomats. Ramses sat on an open courtyard surrounded by bodyguards and watched as envoys from throughout the Middle East laid out offerings of every conceivable kind. Then he would bestow gifts of equal grandeur, proving his largesse and power to himself, his subjects, and the world.

Ramses knew how to use such events to his advantage, and how to portray himself in the best light. He waged one of the most relentless public relations campaigns in history concerning his bravery in the Battle of Kadesh. His use of pomp, ceremony, ritual, and storytelling was masterful.

Ramses II and his young son, Amon-hr-Khopshef, who died young, rope a bull for sacrifice. Temple of Seti 1 at Abydos.

Chapter 21

THE ROYAL SONS — HEIRS TO THE CROWN

One of Ramses' tasks as Pharaoh was to provide for the continuation of his line after his death. The rather short life expectancy meant that this was not at all assured, even if he fathered numerous children. Perhaps Ramses overcompensated with his two hundred children. However, by the time he died at the age of ninety, many of his sons had preceded him in death and the crown fell to an unexpected heir.

Nefertari bore Ramses' first son, Amen-hir-wonwef, and his third, Pre-hir-wonwef. Istnofret was mother of his second, Ramses, and his fourth, Khaemwaset. Ramses designated Amen-hir-wonwef as "Senior king's son" to succeed himself, and took him to Kadesh, where he was sent to the rear to bring up reinforcements. Each of his first fourteen sons accompanied Ramses on a military campaign at a very young age. Nefertari's youngest sons, presumably too young to be considered eligible for the throne, were spared an early introduction to war.

Ramses thought that one of Nefertari's sons would succeed him. However, the accession did not proceed as Ramses hoped. By the time Ramses was forty-five, his eldest son no longer appeared in royal portraits and the brothers nearest his age had died, most in their twenties. Ramses then looked to Nefertari's remaining sons for an heir-designate, rejecting one and finally appointing his younger brother heir. However, this son, too, soon died.

Ramses then turned to Istnofret's oldest, the young Ramses, now in his mid-twenties. Ramses served as heir-designate for nearly a quarter of a century, but could not outlive his father. In the end, Merenptah, the thirteenth son of Ramses' second consort, ascended to the throne. He was in his sixties at his father's death.

Of all his children, the one who achieved the most was Istnofret's Khaemwaset, Ramses' fourth son. Khaemwaset was introduced to war as early as Ramses's other children; however, he had little interest in pursuing a military career, and instead became a scholar and philosopher.

Khaemwaset was often depicted with Ramses taking part in religious rites. Ramses appointed Khaemwaset Second Chief Priest of Ptah when he was in his twenties, a very young age for such an honor. The Prince was in charge of the sacred bulls of Ptah. In the course of performing his duties he devised a new arrangement for burying each sacred bull when it died. The bulls had been entombed in the desert rock, with small chapels built above to contain offerings of statuettes and amulets.

Khaemwaset struck upon the idea of building a long gallery of burial chambers. This simple idea helped to preserve his name in history, for the gallery was still in use one thousand years later. Khaemwaset's name is still prominent upon the walls. Khaemwaset became legendary as a scholar and magician. In the first century A.D., he figured prominently in two stories. In one he had seen the judgment halls of the netherworld and had won the god's Book of Wisdom in a board game. In another his son had saved Egypt from Nubian conquest by banishing an ancient spirit.

Khaemwaset followed his father's lead in the restoration of the ancient and sacred relics from the Egyptian past. Dedicating his efforts to his father, he restored the pyramids of the kings of the Old Kingdom, including that of Cheops of Giza. He served his father in several different capacities, as administrator, priest, archaeologist, and personal aide — even as heir-apparent for a few years just before his death.

Khaemwaset was the last of Ramses' descendants for many generations who was able to match his father's leadership qualities. From Ramses' death onward there was a decline in the pharaohs' control over the forces of disintegration. Merenptah, Ramses' heir, was unable to prevent revolts in both Libya and Nubia. Although he won several important battles against outside invaders, Ramses III was plagued by strikes among his own workers. The last of the Ramsesside dynasty, Ramses XI, died approximately one hundred and fifty years after the burial of Ramses II, having lost control of Nubia to his own viceroy. Soon thereafter Egypt became a loose confederation of the northern and southern states. By then teams of looters were destroying the great tombs and their works of art, legacies of Egypt's past.

Chapter 22

THE FESTIVALS OF JUBILEE

Ramses did not foresee the fate of his descendants, and in fact was filled with assurance that he and his line would continue indefinitely. To assure that his own powers would be prolonged, he celebrated the traditional Egyptian Jubilee, or Festival of Renewal. The jubilee had been a practice of every pharaoh who had reigned for thirty years or more. Each pharaoh's first jubilee was celebrated in his thirtieth year, with others following periodically until the end of his reign. In each festival the king was symbolically recrowned and thus renewed his command of the blessings and allegiance of his subjects.

Ramses started preparing for his first jubilee long before his thirtieth year as Pharaoh. Although tradition had dictated that Memphis be the host city, Ramses decided to celebrate the festival instead at his beloved Pi-Ramses. He erected a huge hall of columns, thirty feet high, with a granite gateway forty feet high. Inside the building and entranceway were obelisks and massive statues of the Pharaoh. He added numerous others as the years went by.

In deference to tradition, Ramses sent Khaemwaset in his official role as Assistant Priest to Memphis to proclaim the jubilee. Khaemwaset, accompanied by a large retinue, then visited every major city along his route, making public pronouncement of the upcoming event and leaving memorials wherever he went.

The ceremony of the Jubilee had its roots in ancient history. It was lengthy and formal, including mystical elements that were unfamiliar to the people of the day. Symbolism and ritual were very important parts of the celebration. A major symbol was the huge pillar erected during the month prior to the anniversary of Ramses' accession to the throne. The pillar symbolized stability and the continuation of the pharaoh's reign throughout time.

During the first month of the jubilee high officials presented themselves to the king while symbolic as well as real preparations were being made. On his anniversary day, Ramses reenacted his crowning before his family, priests, and subjects. A huge feast and theatrical presentation followed. The king's reign over united Upper and Lower Egypt was strengthened as priests from every part of the country brought regional offerings to contribute to the ceremony. Ramses emphasized his solidarity with the gods by commissioning a series of statues of himself standing together with gods of almost every locality in Egypt.

On the same day, symbolic crownings were held in temples in Memphis and other cities. Many workers took time off to attend the festivals. They saw the event as a harbinger of good weather and abundant crops for the year to come. It was a time of good spirits and high morale.

Ramses' first jubilee marked the end of his role as leader on the battlefield. Although he had not entered into any major battles after the Hittite peace, there had been some skirmishes with pirates and rebel tribes. However, after his thirtieth year, Ramses no longer accompanied his troops on these exploits. He was content to stay home with his family and leave military affairs to others.

Ramses spent a great deal of time in the following years celebrating additional Jubilee ceremonies. They became more frequent as the years passed by, often one festival every two years. Altogether Ramses celebrated at least thirteen and possibly fourteen jubilees, more than any other pharaoh.

Statues of Ramses II in the Court of Ramses II, Temple of Amun, Luxor Temple. On the right, Ramses II is shown as Osiris, god of resurrection. The columns are in the form of the closed lotus bud.

Chapter 23

RAMSES' DEATH

Egyptians did not automatically revere old age in itself. However, great admiration was reserved for those who achieved advanced years with a youthful appearance. There was a great market for medicines designed to slow the aging process and delay graying. Ramses was a vigorous man. While he was in his eighties, he energetically celebrated jubilees and took an active role in government. However, as he grew older he stayed more often within the walls of his palace. His country was comparatively prosperous and at peace, requiring little more from him.

On August of his ninetieth year, at the height of the summer heat, Ramses died at Pi-Ramses. An official proclamation of death was made and his son Merenptah began preparations for his burial, just as Ramses himself had done sixty-five years earlier for his father.

In some ways we know more about the Egyptians in death than in life, for the remains and relics of their tombs have been well preserved through history. Perhaps this is fitting, for to Egyptians life was merely a preparation for the new life to come, a testing ground before judgment.

Ramses was well-prepared for his new existence. He, like all Egyptians, believed that happiness was not assured after death, but must be earned, even by a pharaoh. The Egyptians believed they would be judged prior to their entrance into the afterworld, and that happiness thereafter depended at least partially upon how carefully their tombs had been prepared.

The Book Of The Dead describes in detail the process through which Egyptians believed they would go. First, they would appear before their judge, listing the sins from which they had refrained during their lifetimes. The list included such deeds as treating others poorly, driving others to work beyond their strength, lying, and neglecting children. The dead then addressed an additional forty-two gods, again denying the commission of sins. Finally, each petitioner's heart was placed on a scale, opposite a statue of truth. If the heart weighed true, the petitioner was admitted to the peace of the afterworld.

Most people believed that very few, if any, were sinless. They counted on their good deeds to outweigh their bad deeds. However, some few declared themselves to have achieved acceptance by the gods before death. We do not know whether Ramses counted himself in this group. However, he declared his High Priest of Amun to be among the elect, and it seems unlikely that he would be presumptuous enough to bless someone else with this honor if he did not feel that he had acquired it first.

All pharaohs spent a great deal of time preparing their tombs to ensure an easy transit to a happy new world. Ramses was diligent in preparing for his death. He, like his father and grandfather, chose to be buried in the Valley of the Kings, a valley located within the cliffs of the mountains west of Thebes. There he would join a long succession of pharaohs.

The valley's isolated location was thought to be a protection against looters who had removed most of the valuables buried in earlier, more accessible tombs. Kings of the newer dynasties wanted to keep their burial spots intact forever, and ordered their workmen to excavate long hallways leading to burial chambers. Some tombs were as much as one hundred yards deep into the mountain. The location of each tomb was kept a secret to protect the king's integrity in the next life.

The royal tombs were cut directly into the limestone rock. Workers used copper and bronze picks to dig out the rock, which was carried away in baskets. The corridors leading to the tombs were plastered, then images and inscriptions drawn on them. These images were then carved into the rock and painted. When the corridor was too deep for the sunlight to penetrate, lamps made of salted oil and cloth wicks were used to illuminate the work. The pharaohs' tombs were not built to be visited after burial; they were closed and remained unopened until either looters or later civilizations discovered them. However, the workmanship was just as fine as for a temple which would be used and viewed for hundreds of years.

Ramses' tomb did not contain the inscriptions found on many commoners' or even nobles' tombs. He did not list his good or bad deeds, did not deny sins, and did not implore the gods to watch over him. Instead, he ordered the walls of his tomb inscribed with the sacred books of the day, descriptions of myths and rites of the greater gods of Egypt. When he appeared in inscriptions, he was already accepted by the gods as one of them.

Ramses' tomb, like all of the others, began with a long corridor leading to a waiting hall. Further along the corridor was a hall in which he ordered his chariots to be placed. Beyond this room was still another hall and finally the burial room itself. To the side of the burial vault were two rooms which served as resting spots for the gods.

Ramses ordered numerous accouterments for his tomb. No pharaoh could be without a mask made of gold, a highly-decorated sarcophagus, jewelry, sandals, walking sticks, scepters, and other indications of his royalty.

When Ramses died, Merenptah had seventy days to complete the burial arrangements. Many had been made long before — the tomb had probably been finished for years, the work overseen with great care by Ramses himself. However, mummification rites remained to be completed, and the sarcophagus and its decorations finished. Ramses' personal belongings had to be collected, sorted and transported to the tomb.

Ramses' funeral cortege was massive. His servants carried his personal belongings, cakes and flowers in solemn procession behind the high priests and members of his family. The casket was hidden behind curtains in an ox-drawn funeral cart. Egyptians were very emotional at funerals, and relatives following the bier wept openly for their loss.

The final rites included both priest and family. Before the tomb was entered, priests put a small cone on the sarcophagus, similar to those used in celebrations or parties. As the group made its way through the corridors, rituals were conducted to restore Ramses' hearing, sight, taste and movement. Finally, Ramses was laid in his burial vault, accompanied by his chariot, his bed and the momentos he had cherished throughout his life. The tomb was sealed and covered with rubble to hide its location. Ramses was, his survivors believed, safe in his new home.

Every funeral was followed by a funeral feast. Such feasts began with assurances that the dead were doing well in their new home, and with reminders of the cycle of life and man's brief stay on earth. Then there was eating, drinking and remembrance of the one departed.

Ramses was not considered to be entirely absent even after his death. His survivors assumed that he knew the events of their lives and could intervene to help them when needed. Since his name was tied to theirs, their ruin would be his sorrow. In times of trouble he would often be called upon to come to the aid of those he had loved.

The Temple of Ramses II at Abydos

Chapter 24

THE SUMMING UP

Ramses' life was rich and full of experience. A warrior at an early age, a young husband with a regal wife, a man of great bravery in a situation others would call hopeless, a great builder and peacemaker — Ramses was all of these. Shelley was to scorn his might in the great poem "Ozymandias."

I met a traveler from an antique land
Who said: "Two vast and trunkless legs of stone
Stand in the desert . . . Near them, on the sand,
Half-sunk, a shattered visage lies, whose frown,
And wrinkled lip, and sneer of cold command,
Tell that its sculptor well those passions read
Which yet survive, stamped on these lifeless things,
The hand that mocked them, and the heart that fed.
And on the pedestal these words appear:
'My name is Ozymandias, King of Kings:
Look on my works, ye Mighty, and despair!'
Nothing beside remains. Round the decay
Of that colossal wreck, boundless and bare,
The lone and level sands stretch far away."

And yet Ramses' fame has outlasted the ruins of his statues. His life is another guidepost in man's search for what makes a society — and its rulers — strong. Ramses was able to do what few of his peers could — establish order, keep his country united, and give his people that most prized of possessions, peace. Within the mysteries of Egyptian civilization remains a man who speaks to us of pride, courage, and the human qualities that are eternal.